THINK AGAIN

To my family and all the children all over the world. May we learn to appreciate each other
for who we REALLY are — DEF

I dedicate this book to all of my family, especially to my wife, Teresa, and my kids, Chris and Ashley,
for dealing with all my late night work sessions. I love you. And to the world . . .
"We all CAN get along" — JB

The text type was set in Compacta.
Book design by Steven Scott.

Text and illustrations copyright © 2002 by ONE GAZILLION, INC.
All rights reserved. Published by Scholastic Inc.
Printed in the U.S.A.

ISBN 0-439-56716-5

3 4 5 6 7 8 9 10   23   12 11 10 09 08 07

HIP KID HOP
THINK AGAIN

by Doug E. Fresh

Illustrated by Joseph Buckingham Jr.

SCHOLASTIC INC.

New York   Toronto   London   Auckland   Sydney   Mexico City   New Delhi   Hong Kong   Buenos Aires

There was a new kid in school and his name was Zack. Now Zack was the talk of the class because he was black.

Sitting next to Zack was a kid named John, who was known in school to have it going on.

The school that they went to was mostly white,
and because of their differences the vibe wasn't right.

They hung with
different crews
and they had
different scenes.

Zack wore
brand-name gear,
while John wore
faded jeans.

Zack loved rap with phat beats and rhymes.

John listened to rock to have a good time.

When they tried out
for the basketball team,
they couldn't get along,
they just yelled and screamed.

The coach knew what was up
and that it wasn't cool,
so he pulled them both aside
and kept them after school.

And because of the way they treated each other,
the coach had to call their fathers and mothers.

Both sets of parents came to school that day.
When they heard what happened, here's what they had to say:

"I'm gonna say this once, but you will see it again.
Your worst enemy could be your best friend, so think again."

The coach let them back on the team with one rule—
they would have to clean the gym every day after school.

On that very first day, they didn't want to talk,
so the coach made them write on the board with chalk.

They wrote these words over again and again:
Your worst enemy could be your best friend, so think again.

YOUR WORST ENEMY could BE YOUR BEST FRIEND, So Think Again
YOUR WORST ENEMY could BE YOUR BEST FRIEND, So Think Again
YOUR WORST ENEMY could BE YOUR BEST FRIEND, So Think Again
YOUR WORST ENEMY could BE YOUR BEST FRIEND, So Think Again
YOUR WORST ENEMY could BE YOUR BEST FRIEND, So Think Again
YOUR WORST ENEMY could BE YOUR BEST FRIEND, So Think Again
YOUR WORST ENEMY could BE YOUR BEST FRIEND, So Think Again
YOUR WORST ENEMY could BE YOUR BEST FRIEND, So Think Again
YOUR WORST ENEMY could BE YOUR BEST FRIEND, So Think Again
YOUR WORST ENEMY could BE YOUR BEST FRIEND, So Think Again
YOUR WORST ENEMY could BE YOUR BEST FRIEND, So Think Again

YOUR WORST ENEMY COULD BE YOUR BEST FRIEND So THINK AGAIN
YOUR WORST ENEMY COULD BE YOUR BEST FRIEND So THINK AGAIN
YOUR WORST ENEMY COULD BE YOUR BEST FRIEND So THINK AGAIN
YOUR WORST ENEMY COULD BE YOUR BEST FRIEND So THINK AGAIN
YOUR WORST ENEMY COULD BE YOUR BEST FRIEND So THINK AGAIN
YOUR WORST ENEMY COULD BE YOUR BEST FRIEND So THINK AGAIN
YOUR WORST ENEMY COULD BE YOUR BEST FRIEND So THINK AGAIN
YOUR WORST ENEMY COULD BE YOUR BEST FRIEND So THINK AGAIN
YOUR WORST ENEMY COULD BE YOUR BEST FRIEND So THINK AGAIN
YOUR WORST ENEMY COULD BE YOUR BEST FRIEND So THINK AGAIN
YOUR WORST ENEMY COULD BE YOUR BEST FRIEND So THINK AGAIN
YOUR WORST ENEMY COULD BE YOUR BEST FRIEND So THINK AGAIN

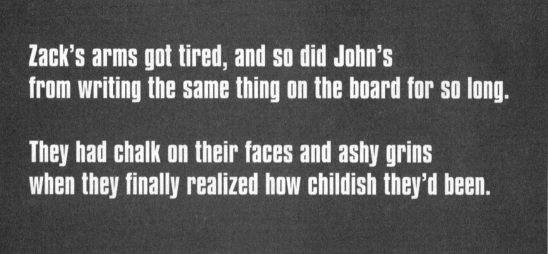

Zack's arms got tired, and so did John's
from writing the same thing on the board for so long.

They had chalk on their faces and ashy grins
when they finally realized how childish they'd been.

For not even talking because of their pride
and not even looking at the real person inside.

And after they learned this in their own special way,
they didn't even mind cleaning the gym every day.

Sweeping and mopping—but making it fun,
laughing and joking while getting it done.

And from that day on, John and Zack were down—
in school, on the phone, hanging out around town.

Playing video games and watching movies on TV,
rapping together and watching BET.

When you saw one of them, you saw the other, and on the basketball team, people called them brothers.

But John's other friends started acting jealous,
'cause he was always with Zack and not the other fellas.

So one day in the locker room when no one was around,
John's old friends tried to push Zack down.

John was outside and felt that something was wrong,
'cause Zack was inside and taking too long.

When John came inside, he couldn't believe his eyes—
Zack was being bullied by a bunch of the guys.

These were his friends, but Zack was, too.
Being violent was something he was not willing to do.

He knew there was a way for them to get along,
so he stepped on the bench and started rapping this song:

Now we have to learn how to treat each other
and never judge anyone based on their color.

We should treat girls like sisters
and guys like brothers.
We can work together and respect one another.

While everyone listened to the words in the song,
they thought, *Maybe he's right, we could all get along.*

Zack stood up as the rap came to an end and said, "Remember, your worst enemy could be your best friend, so think again."